D1486829

Dwayne the Cow

"The Cow that didn't know how…"

By: L. Elvira McKay

Copyright ©2019 by L. Elvira McKay

All Rights Reserved.
No portion of this book may be reproduced or used in any manner whatsoever
without explicit permission in writing from the publisher.

ISBN: 978-1-7327155-1-6 (Paperback Edition)
ISBN: 978-1-7327155-2-3 (eBook Edition)

Written and illustrated by L. Elvira McKay
lelviramckay.com

Special Thanks to *Wendi Moore* for helping me bring my illustrations to life.

Printed in the United States of America
First Edition 2019

10 9 8 7 6 5 4 3 2 1

Dedicated to my beautiful Mother in Heaven

Elvira McKay

"Love Always"

Hello!! I am Dwayne The Cow!

This is my story...

2

Dwayne the Cow was a cow
that didn't know how...

4

The horses knew how.

But Dwayne the Cow
didn't know how…

What did Dwayne the Cow
"not" know how to do??

Dwayne the Cow was a good cow.
He always ate all his chow.

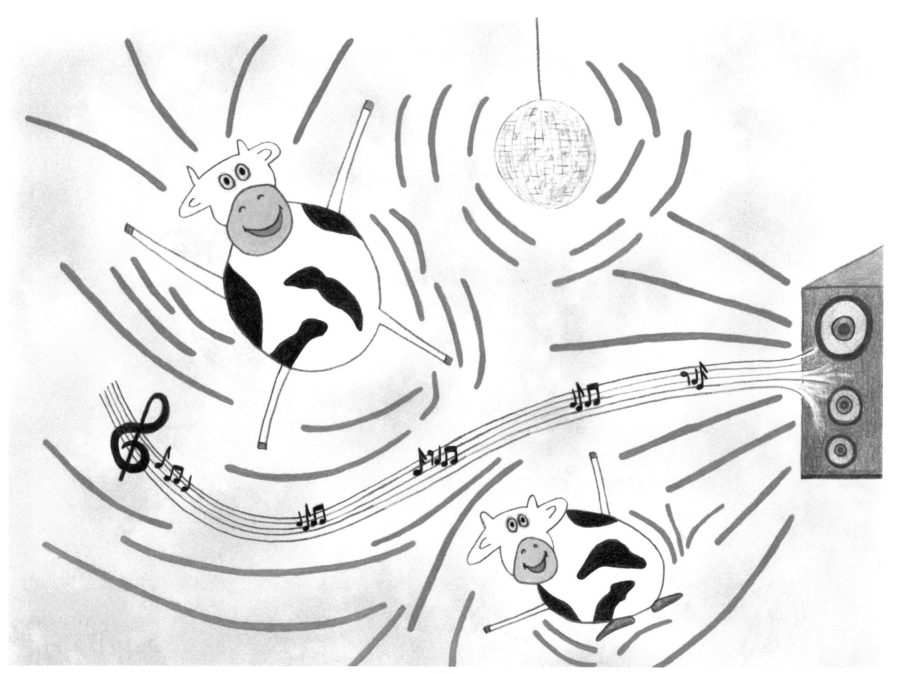

Dwayne the Cow knew how
to *dance* and *sing*!

14

Dwayne the Cow knew how to be a good friend and *"always"* helped others around the farm.

What did Dwayne the Cow
"not" know how to do?

What could it be?

18

Poor Dwayne the Cow.

Dwayne thought he may go insane for he was so plain.

Everyday Dwayne the Cow watched the trains go by and waved to his good friend Zane.

What might it be?

What did Dwayne the Cow
not know how to do?

Day after day the sun would shine
brightly and at night the stars would
burst across the sky, yet Dwayne
the Cow didn't know how...

As the seasons changed, Dwayne the
Cow looked to GOD and prayed.

For Dwayne the Cow didn't know how...

In his *heart* he knew that in
time he would know how...

One day it rained.

There was so much rain,
the plain had to be drained.

Dwayne the Cow remained
on the plain in the rain.

It just *rained* and *rained!!!*

The horses rejoiced with gladness
that day it rained.

What made them so happy?

Due to the "BIG" rain,
the horses did not plow.

Even though they knew how.

Dwayne the Cow wanted to plow,
but he didn't know how.

The next day, after the rain,
the horses were sold.

40

Who was going to plow?

Thought Dwayne the Cow.

Who could help the farmer plow?

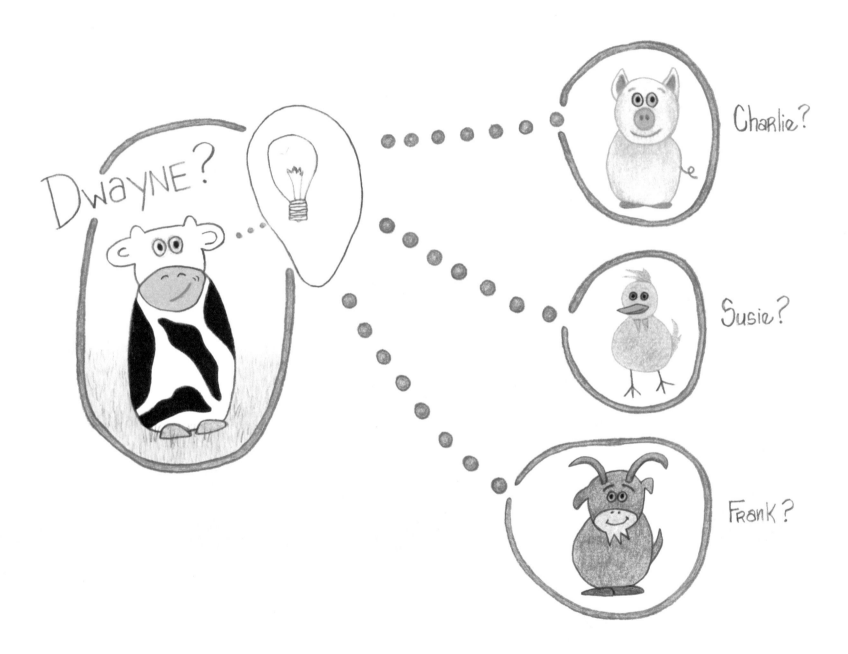

Maybe someone on the farm that
really wanted to plow???!!!

46

But who?

Just who could it be?

DWAYNE

48

Dwayne the Cow was
going to plow!!!!!!!!!!

The farmer would teach Dwayne how.

Dwayne the Cow
no longer felt plain or insane.

Now he was "DWAYNE THE COW, THE COW THAT KNEW HOW TO PLOW!!!!!"

Love you!!

Like Dwayne the Cow, you can learn anything and everything you desire.

All you need is to be willing to learn, have faith in GOD and know in your heart that you will succeed.

Matthew 19:26 –   JESUS looked at them and said,
"With man this is impossible, but with GOD all things are possible."

Author Bio

L. Elvira McKay
Called to write.

Dwayne the Cow is a character I created while attending high school in Cinnaminson, N.J. Dwayne always held a special place in my heart. He was affectionately charming and kind. I kept the book, put it in a folder and promptly moved on with my life. Life moved me to Northport, Alabama. A town with the distinction of being located across the river from Tuscaloosa. Home to the University of Alabama (Roll Tide!!!). One day I was looking at the book and decided to finish and publish it so that I could share Dwayne the Cow with others. My hope was that Dwayne the Cow could bring children closer to GOD. An opportunity for kids to learn that although life has many challenges, with GOD in their lives, the possibilities to succeed are endless and amazing. All they need to do is persevere and believe. Enjoy Dwayne the Cow and look forward to more adventures to come.

CPSIA information can be obtained
at www.ICGtesting.com
Printed in the USA
BVHW092131151019
561214BV00001B/1/P